Summer Housing Boy

SHORT STORIES OF A CITY KID

Written By Shaniqua Lewis
Illustrated By Ninakupenda Gaillard

For More Information:

Email:
Shaniqua@divineworks.org

If you would like to purchase books for your classroom or
in bulk please email shaniqua@divineworks.org
with the subject line: SHB Bulk Order.

To purchase books or products please visit our website at:
www.shaniqualewis.com

ISBN:
978-0-578-54912

This book is dedicated to
my brothers
Justin and Mikhial,
I love you both
and a little more
when it is necessary.

Hi! My name is Tyreek. Everyone calls me Reek, but we don't know each other very well, so let's start with names. Hopefully, we can become friends. Let me show you around my neighborhood. First, this is my home. I live waaayy up on the 5th floor with my family and my pet dog,"Pancha."

Did I mention I love summer? Here is Mr. Joe. He is one of the maintenance workers who keeps our buildings and parks clean. I don't think he prefers the summer; his mustache is always right side up when we run on his neat grass. I always want to tell Mr. Joe; that he should put his tidy leaves in a bag while he's cleaning. It's tough for us kids to tell the difference between his finished pile of leaves and the grass on the ground. Let me get back to my discussion explaining why I love summer! In July, my skin becomes multiple shades of brown, with a hint of darkened russet, reddish-brown. Being outside is also liberating. We get to scream with laughter, it's so much fun! Out of nowhere, the leaves begin swirling into miniature tornado's, right before a summer storm! What could go wrong?

WORMMS, that's what!

The water cycle in science class didn't prepare me for what happens after precipitation, condensation, and evaporation. There was so much rain that the underground creatures got ejected out. Now, there are huge worms everywhere! I can't stand those slimy, sleek, puny yet enormous worms!!! Pancha is my best friend, but she isn't much help with creepy crawling insects or anything else for that matter.

Come meet some of my adult friends:
Here's Greg, he walks his huge dog every morning with the same expressionless face and sandals.

 Meet Ms. Mother and her daughter Alexis. She drops Alexis off to camp on her way to work.

 Last but not least, meet Mr. Poepoe. I don't know his real name but mama always tells me to say a prayer for Mr. Poepoe at night; so I do.

Ms.Mother is one of my favorite people in the whole wide world. She is always kind to me. Ms. Mother always tells me I am going to be someone important when I grow up. Needless to say, I believe her. I wonder why she says these things to me, and not everyone else in the neighborhood. Some days I find myself wanting to ask her, "how can I be great?"

Summer is here, summer is here, summer is here! I love going to the water park during the summer. But sometimes my family can't afford to go so we make water slides! I help build water slides for our neighborhood. Mama says I'm going to be a great inventor one day. Since the slides are a bit rusty and the floor is hot, I bring buckets to the slides. We usually fill the buckets up with water and run the water down the slide. We have the most fun pretending we are at the water park! Cool, right? Yeah, I know!

My friends and I call ourselves the Wolf Pack, we are super smart and we stick together! Say hi to Mikki, Imani, Jon Jon, Ramel, and Jamiliah. Jamiliah is my best friend, and she is also one of the most skilled basketball players in our neighborhood!

Sadly nobody picks her when separating teams for basketball because she is a girl, but whenever I play, I always pick my best friend, and we always win!

After the park, I always hear a loud, rumbling noise from my stomach--so I take my wet money and go to my favorite corner store, Baba's. They make the best sandwiches with a special sauce straight from Heaven. Mama tells me to save my money and eat food from upstairs, but my stomach never seems to make it that far!

YUUMMMM, now let's head to Mama.....

My mom rushes me upstairs so that I can take a shower and change, before her Zerobics class! I think that's how you say it! Mama says I walk too slow, but I think she walks too fast! I think she walks fast because of her Zerobics classes. There are always strong women in her Zerobics classes. All the ladies from the neighborhood come together for the class to sweat and dance.

* Tyreek is unfamiliar with the word Aerobics,so instead he says Zerobics.

After Zerobic's class, I always ask my mom for ice cream or an icy from the little old lady on the corner. My mom always asks if I want to use my chore money. Though I always want ice cream, I never want to use my own money.

After class, Mama likes to eat a whole lot of green stuff, she calls it healthy food! It takes us 40-minutes to get from our building to the farmers market. We always take the bus.
It's a pretty long ride, but because the food is so good, it's worth it. On our way there I love to stare at the shapes and colors of the houses,each neighborhood has a unique look.

Meet my family, here is Mama, Pops, my baby sister Sapphire, and Pancha of course! Pancha loves to eat momma's delicious healthy green food, so I sneak her some once in a while.
But shhhhh, don't tell Mama!

I think I can call you a friend now.
Friend,I know I will achieve greatness one day.
Every night I draw what I see. If I see a building, I draw it. If I see a house, I draw it. If I see huge skyscrapers, I also draw them. Can I let you in on a secret? I know one day my family and I are going to move out of this building. Soon, I will be able to not only draw that neighborhood, but own it too.

I can picture my dream house right now. It has five rooms, three bathrooms and all the healthy green food you can eat. It also has a grill in the backyard beside my outdoor pool. The healthy food market won't be a 40-minute bus ride away. It will be in the neighborhood. I can't wait to invite you, the Wolf Pack, Ms. Mother, & Alexis over to my very own home. It's going to be spectacular friend.
Can't wait for you to see it!

The End

Tyreek's Wall of Definitions

Precipitation- the act of water falling in the form of rain, snow, sleet, or hail.

Condensation- Condensation is a change in the state of water from a gas or vapor form into liquid form.
For example,eye glasses fogging up when you enter a warm building on a cold winter day, or water drops forming on a glass holding a cold drink on a hot summer day.

Evaporation- is when a liquid becomes a gas without forming bubbles inside the liquid volume.
For example, water left in a bowl will slowly disappear.
The water evaporates into water vapor, the gas phase of water.
The water vapor mixes with the air.

Miniature - a very small copy or model of something.
For example, he bought a miniature of his favorite car.

Expressionless- (of a person's face or voice) not conveying any emotion; unemotional.

Zerobics aka Aerobics- is a vigorous exercise, such as swimming or walking, designed to strengthen the heart and lungs.

Shaniqua Lewis is a Christian author that was inspired to write her first book after she was diagnosed with Adult ADHD at the age of 23. As a former collegiate basketball and volleyball player, she struggled academically but kept pushing herself to do well.

Her late diagnosis helped her understand many of her prior difficulties in school. She wants to inspire children with similar challenges to go beyond the boundaries of their diagnosis.

She graduated with a Bachelor's degree from the illustrious Virginia Union University and is pursuing a Master's Degree in Industrial-Organizational Psychology.

Her former job was an Educational Specialist. In that role, she advocated for parents and children with learning differences by developing IEP's (Individual Educational Plans) and helping them engage other support services from their schools.

She is the founder of Divine Works, an international art ministry that produces short films and art shows.

Shaniqua is dedicated to inspiring others to push beyond their circumstances, diagnosis, and difficulties and to use their God-given creative abilities to make room. Even with her diagnosis, she wrote a book and published it, and you can too!

CPSIA information can be obtained
at www.ICGtesting.com
Printed in the USA
LVRC021338040220
645807LV00001B/2

9 780578 549125